A Home that Means the WORLD

To my aunts ~ Jane, Jo, Linda,
Lorna, and Rosemary

A Home that Means the World © 2024 Quarto Publishing plc.
Text and illustrations © Victoria Turnbull 2024.
First Published in 2024 by Frances Lincoln Children's Books, an imprint of The Quarto Group.
100 Cummings Center, Suite 265D, Beverly, MA 01915, USA.
T +1 978-282-9590 F +1 078-283-2742 **www.Quarto.com**

A CIP record for this book is available from the Library of Congress.
ISBN 978-0-71126-232-4

The illustrations were created with graphite and colored pencil
Set in Bellota

Designer: Zoë Tucker
Production Controller: Dawn Cameron
Art Director: Karissa Santos
Publisher: Peter Marley

Manufactured in Guangdong, China TT062024
9 8 7 6 5 4 3 2 1

Victoria Turnbull

A Home
that Means the
WORLD

Frances Lincoln
Children's Books

The house was in a tree
that gave shelter and shade,
and branches for Flora
to swing on.

It was small and it was held together by thread, but it meant the world to the Weavers.

The Weavers were ants.
Flora's mother wove to furnish their home.
She wove rugs and blankets and cushions.

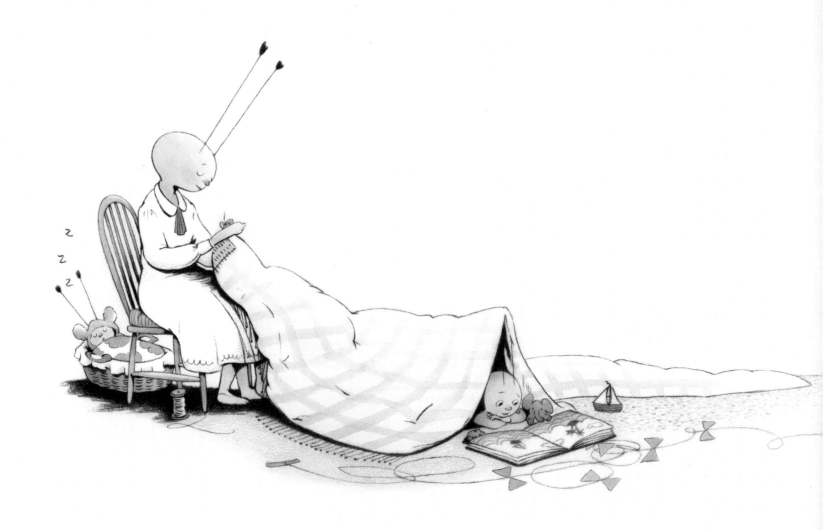

When the weavings grew threadbare,
Flora's mother mended them.

Until one day,

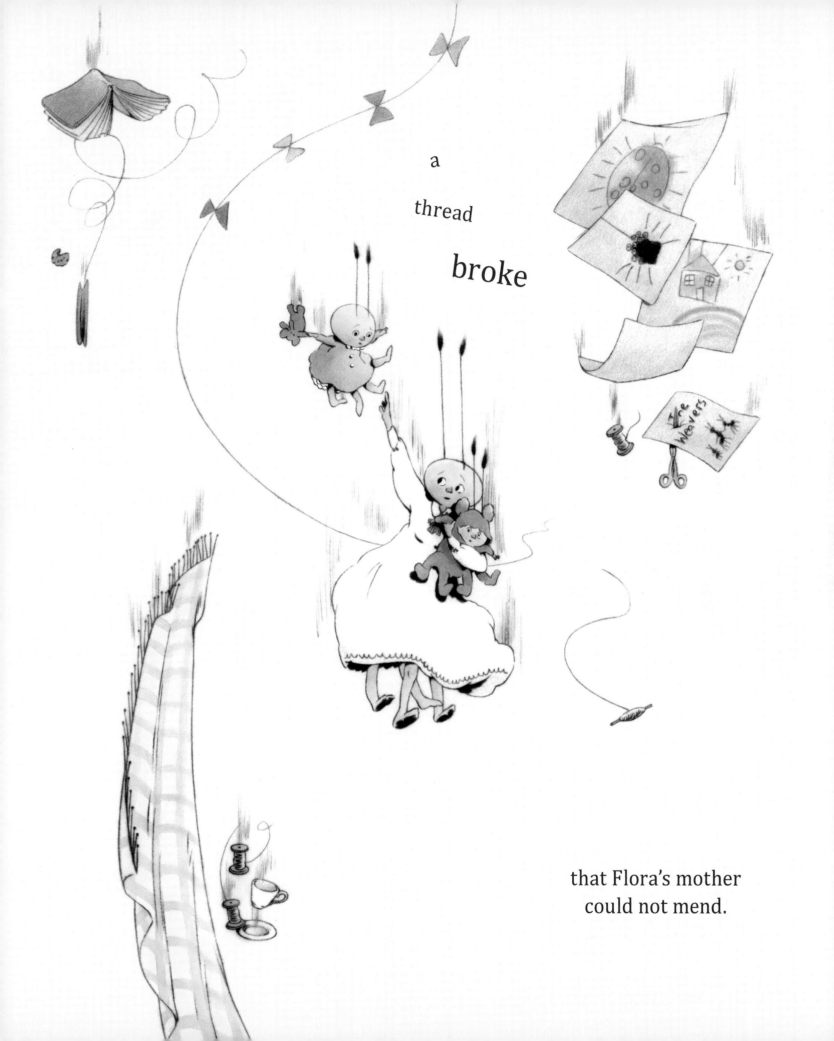

a

thread

broke

that Flora's mother
could not mend.

The Weavers bundled up what was left of their home...

... and set off in search of another.

On the way, Flora discovered
they were not alone. There were
those who had journeys of
their own to make...

... and those who had stories
of their own to tell.

Then there were those who couldn't understand them at all.

The Weavers kept moving.

Days went by.

Some days the world was kind.

Some days the world was not.

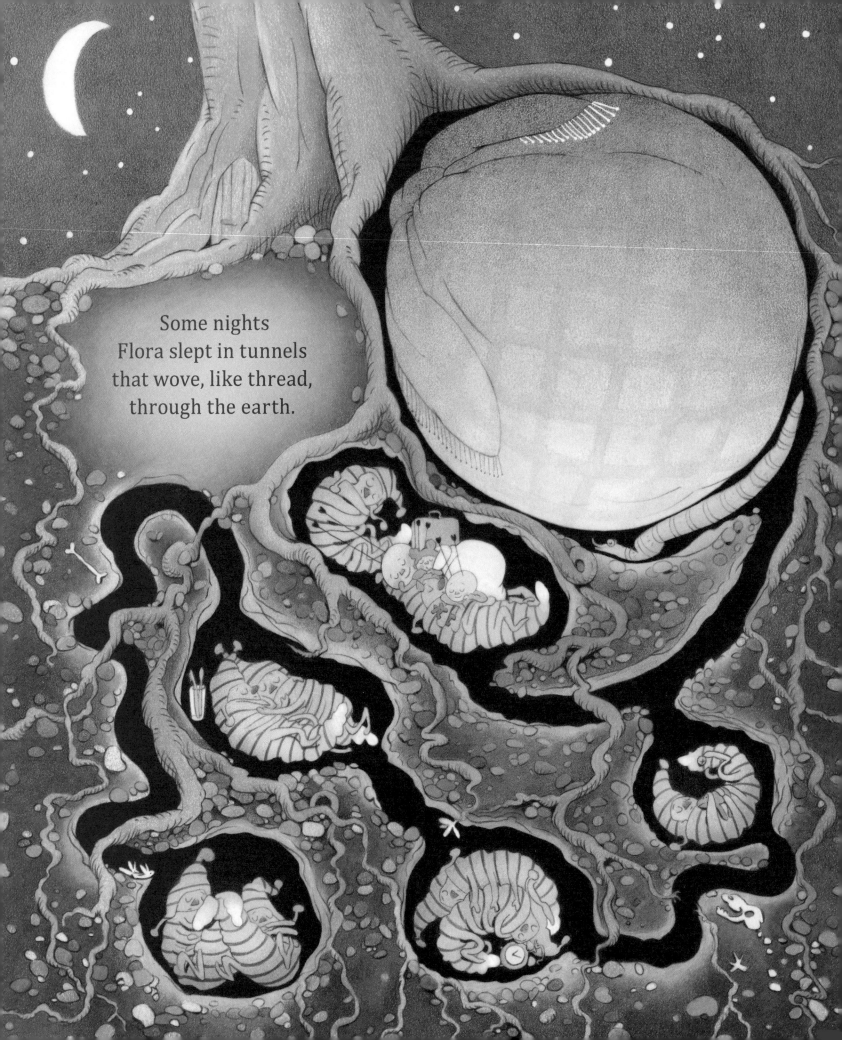

Some nights
Flora slept in tunnels
that wove, like thread,
through the earth.

Others she spent sleepless under stars.

Flora slept and woke.

She felt sun

and wind

and rain.

And every day she searched the horizon
for something small that might grow into a home.

Eventually the Weavers came to a city.
But on the crowded streets,
their voices went unheard.

Once more they had to move on,
only this time Flora's mother didn't
know which way to go.

They were lost.

But lost can be found,

broken can mend.

And with a little help, Flora found
that what had been closed...

... could open again.

This is Flora's home now.

It is small and it is held together
by thread, but it means the world
to the Weavers...

... and to any visitors that arrive.